Dear Parents:

Congratulations! Your child is taking the first steps on an exciting journey. The destination? Independent reading!

STEP INTO READING® will help your child get there. The program offers five steps to reading success. Each step includes fun stories and colorful art or photographs. In addition to original fiction and books with favorite characters, there are Step into Reading Non-Fiction Readers, Phonics Readers and Boxed Sets, Sticker Readers, and Comic Readers—a complete literacy program with something to interest every child.

Learning to Read, Step by Step!

Ready to Read   Preschool–Kindergarten
• big type and easy words • rhyme and rhythm • picture clues
For children who know the alphabet and are eager to begin reading.

Reading with Help   Preschool–Grade 1
• basic vocabulary • short sentences • simple stories
For children who recognize familiar words and sound out new words with help.

Reading on Your Own   Grades 1–3
• engaging characters • easy-to-follow plots • popular topics
For children who are ready to read on their own.

Reading Paragraphs   Grades 2–3
• challenging vocabulary • short paragraphs • exciting stories
For newly independent readers who read simple sentences with confidence.

Ready for Chapters   Grades 2–4
• chapters • longer paragraphs • full-color art
For children who want to take the plunge into chapter books but still like colorful pictures.

STEP INTO READING® is designed to give every child a successful reading experience. The grade levels are only guides; children will progress through the steps at their own speed, developing confidence in their reading.

Remember, a lifetime love of reading starts with a single step!

Copyright © 2020 Disney Enterprises, Inc. Published in the United States by Random House Children's Books, a division of Penguin Random House LLC, 1745 Broadway, New York, NY 10019, and in Canada by Penguin Random House Canada Limited, Toronto, in conjunction with Disney Enterprises, Inc.

Step into Reading, Random House, and the Random House colophon are registered trademarks of Penguin Random House LLC.

Visit us on the Web!
StepIntoReading.com
rhcbooks.com

Educators and librarians, for a variety of teaching tools, visit us at RHTeachersLibrarians.com

ISBN 978-0-7364-4112-4 (trade) — ISBN 978-0-7364-8299-8 (lib. bdg.)
ISBN 978-0-7364-4121-6 (ebook)

Printed in the United States of America

10 9 8 7 6 5 4 3 2

Mulan's Happy Panda

by Amy Sky Koster

illustrated by the Disney Storybook Art Team

Random House New York

Blossom is a panda.

Her tummy rumbles.

She is hungry.

Blossom runs

to a nearby town.

She crawls under
the gate.

The town is
having a party!
It is the Moon Festival.

Blossom sees tables
covered with food.
She reaches
for something to eat.

Someone scares her.

She runs away!

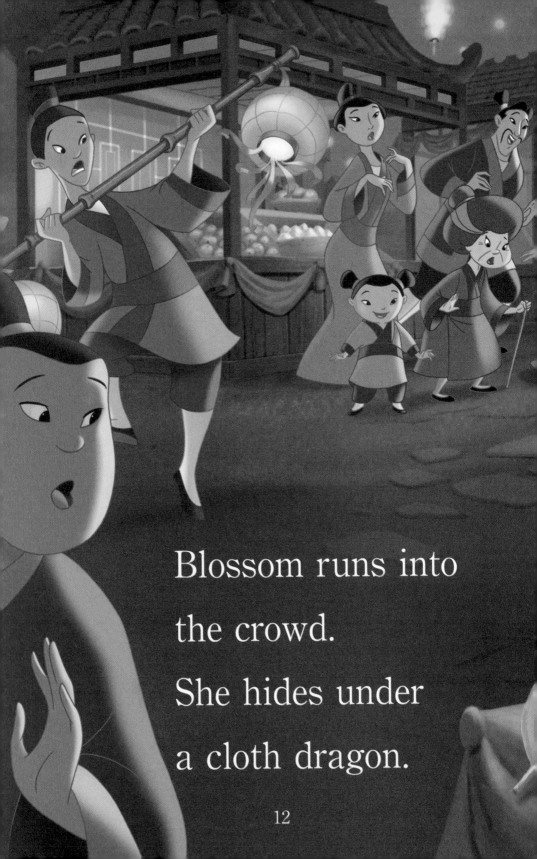

Blossom runs into
the crowd.
She hides under
a cloth dragon.

12

Blossom dances
in the parade!

But everyone leaves
when they see Blossom.
They are afraid
of bears!

Blossom finds more food.

Mulan is at the table!

Mulan and Blossom
both reach for cake.
The cakes fall!

Mulan looks at Blossom.
She thinks the panda
is very cute!

Mulan picks Blossom up.

She invites Blossom
to live with her!

Mulan takes Blossom
to see the lanterns.
Blossom is happy!

Blossom
loves Mulan!